CW00386152

Willow

by
Alex Martin

Book Four of the

KATHERINE WHEEL SERIES

A CHILDHOOD INTERLUDE
Summer 1934

ACKNOWLEDGEMENTS

I am indebted to my son and editor, Dr Tomas L Martin. He insisted a novella to bridge the gap between the generations in The Katherine Wheel Series would always be needed, and eventually I caved in. As usual, he was right.

Thanks go to Jane Dixon-Smith of http://www.jdsmith-design.com/ for her sensitive interpretation of my ideas for the cover.

Always, my thanks to Phil for his endless patience.

Please go to www.intheplottingshed.com for further information about The Katherine Wheel Series and other books by Alex Martin

CHAPTER ONE

Lottie

"Hello, anyone home?" Lottie Flintock-Smythe leaned her dark head out of the window of the old Sunbeam saloon as it swept into the forecourt of Katherine Wheel Garage. "Toot the horn, Mummy!"

To her delight, her mother, Cassandra, obliged with a long blast of her horn.

"I don't think anyone's about." Lottie started clambering out of the car. "But I'll find Al, you'll see."

"Be careful, Lottie, I haven't even parked yet!" Cassandra yanked on the handbrake and came to a full-stop but Lottie was already running into the workshop, housed in an old Nissen hut left over from the war and situated behind the petrol pumps.

"Can I go too, Mummy?" Isobel, always more obedient than her older sister, piped up from the back of the car.

"No, you stay with me, young lady. One of you running off is bad enough."

Isobel waited patiently until her mother opened the door of the car. They walked to the forecourt shop together, hand-in-hand. No-one was there, not even Lottie.

"Honestly, it's no way to run a business. What if we were a customer wanting petrol?" Cassandra peered into the office behind the shop.

"Found him!" Lottie burst in, triumphantly presenting her mother with her best friend, Al Phipps, the son of the proprietors of the garage, Katy and Jem.

"Hello, Aunt Cassandra. Are you looking for Mum? She's in the factory." Al nodded his chestnut wavy hair in the direction of the new industrial building on the other side of the forecourt.

1

"Yes, Al, I am. How are you today?"

Lottie nudged him in the ribs to remind him of his manners. It seemed especially important to be polite today, with her mother dressed up in her best coat and hat, a fur stole around her slim shoulders, all smartened up for her trip to London.

Al obediently replied. "Very well, thank you. And you?"

Lottie beamed her pleasure.

Cassandra smiled back. "I'm fine, Al, but I'm in a bit of a hurry. I must catch the train to London and it's due in half an hour. It was so hard to get away from Lady Smythe this morning, it's made me late."

"Come on, I'll show you where Mum is. She's up to her eyes in work. Been at it since dawn, Dad said. Some big order's come in, you see, and Dad says it could make all the difference to us keeping the factory going." Al was already marching out of the office-come-shop and over to the rubber factory. A pungent smell emanated from its drab exterior.

"That's good, Al, and I'm glad to hear it, but does that mean my girls can't stay with you today?"

"Dunno, have to ask my mum."

Lottie knew a moment of panic. "Oh, Mummy, do say we can stay, please. It's so boring up at the manor without the others." She gave her sister a meaningful look.

Although so different, both in looks and personalities, the two sisters always understood each other when dealing with authority. They'd had plenty of practice with their grandmother, Lady Smythe, the disciplinarian of their home, Cheadle Manor. Lottie resembled her in many ways, with her robust body and sharp brain, which she ruthlessly exploited to her advantage, knowing she was Granny's favourite simply because they shared a common bond in their ability to command. Her sister had a different approach. Isobel was blonde and pretty and quiet. Everyone said she was more like their late father's side of the family, who were all tall, blue-eyed and artistic. Her gentle charm sometimes won the day when Lottie's more forceful approach failed.

Isobel took the hint and joined in with her plea. "Oh, yes, Mummy, don't make us go back home. Granny will keep us indoors all day and it's so sunny and warm."

Lottie looked at her mother, who had pursed her lips in a tell-tale sign that she wasn't happy but wasn't going to say why.

They reached the factory building and pushed open the heavy door.

"Cooee!" Cassandra called out.

Lottie peered into the cavernous space and inhaled the peculiar smell of rubber. She didn't mind it, not really, but it was very odd. Almost exotic. She knew it came from a place called Malaya which was very far away but couldn't imagine what it must be like there. One day, she and Al would go there together, like real explorers, and visit the rubber plantations Aunt Katy had told them about.

Katy Phipps, wearing her habitual grease-stained dungarees and bright headscarf tied up on top of her dark curls, came out from behind an enormous machine with her young daughter, Lily, trailing after her. Lottie thought her mum's friend looked more harassed than ever but sort of excited at the same time.

"Cass! Oh, gosh, I forgot all about having the girls today. You're off to London, aren't you?"

"That's right, Kate. Is there a problem? Only, I'm in an awful rush if I'm to catch the ten o'clock train." Cassandra gave her friend a perfunctory kiss, then glanced down at her wristwatch. A glint of diamonds from its jewelled bracelet sparkled in the summer sunshine.

"Um, no, of course not, I know what a treat it is for you to have a trip up to town. Leave them with me, we'll be fine." Katy smiled absently at Lottie and then at Isobel.

"Are you sure? I could take them back to Cheadle Manor. Mother's at home and the housekeeper would at least see they got fed." Cassandra smiled at Lottie too, but Lottie wasn't convinced.

"Please, Aunt Katy, let us stay. I promise we won't get in your way, really we won't." Lottie stared hard at Katy. She wasn't really her aunt, and neither was Cassandra aunt to Al and his kid sister, Lily, but it felt like they were. She couldn't remember them not being part of their everyday lives, except for that bleak time after her father died when her mother had withdrawn from the entire world.

Katy looked searchingly at Cassandra. Then she nodded in her usual decisive way. "Of course, you can, girls. Are you staying overnight, Cass?"

"Yes, in a hotel, which will be hugely expensive, but we have no London house now, so nothing else for it." Cassandra shook her head, making the peacock feather on her matching blue hat quiver.

"Right then, Mrs Flintock-Smythe. Be off with you!" Katy gave Cassandra a gentle push. "Come on, hop in that ancient old bus of yours and get to the station in double-quick time."

"Are you sure?"

"Yes, of course and you'll have to put your foot down or you won't make it."

Lottie's mother laughed, almost giggled, in a way Lottie had not heard for many years. "Alright, alright. I'm going!" She turned to her daughters. "'Bye, darlings. Be good!" Cassandra walked briskly back to the car, got behind the wheel and drove off at top speed.

Katy turned back to the four children. "Right then, you lot. I've got masses to do, so you're going to have to entertain yourselves. Understood? Al's in charge for the day. Is that clear?"

Lottie seethed. She'd just reached fourteen years of age, and she was nine months older than Al. She couldn't keep quiet at that instruction. "We'll be in charge together." She nodded at Al, who grinned back at her.

"Is that alright with you, Al? After all, Bella and Lottie are our guests today, so whatever Lottie may say, I'm holding you responsible."

"Got it, Mum. Don't you worry about us. I know you're under pressure today." Al gave his mother a quick peck on the cheek.

She ruffled his hair. "Go on with you. Yes, I have got a lot on today and, if I get it right, for many days to come. You see, children, a great deal depends on the outcome of my new design, so don't come running to me with trivial problems, and make sure you keep an eye on young Lily too. I've got to concentrate on creating a new mould for this brake component and I don't want to be interrupted. Your Dad's not here, either, Al. He's taken the lorry into Woodbury and Len has gone with him, leaving Uncle Billy to keep things ticking over. I've got to make the most of the peace if we're to stay in business." Katy looked at Lottie. "Understand, Lottie? No interruptions please, or I'll send you packing back to Lady Smythe at the manor."

"Yes, of course I understand, Aunt Katy. We'll be good, I promise. I'll take care of lunch too, if there's stuff in the kitchen?"

"I'm not sure what is in the kitchen, but my mother is bound to have left something, as Agnes probably remembered you were coming, unlike me!" Katy laughed.

"Isn't Grandma in either?" Al asked.

"No, she went with your Dad into Woodbury to see Auntie Maggie. That's why I want you to look after Lily."

"Mum! I'm eight years old now, remember? Stop going on about me being the youngest. I can look after myself." Lily looked outraged. It had been her birthday only two weeks ago. Lottie was surprised Aunt Katy seemed to have forgotten but she was always more interested in machines than people.

"I'm glad to hear it, Lily. Now, I can't waste any more time. Be good, be quiet and leave me alone." With that, Katy disappeared back into the factory and left them to it.

"So, we've got the place to ourselves, it seems." Al squared his shoulders as if taking the weight of responsibility on to them.

Lottie winked at him. "Then let's make the most of it."

CHAPTER TWO
Al

Al had been looking forward to the girls' visit for days. School holidays never lived up to their name for him as he was expected to lend a hand at the garage or the factory. He didn't mind, both were interesting, and he was glad to help his struggling parents. Proud of them too, in their creation of their new businesses, all by themselves. They had started the Katherine Wheel Garage just after the Great War, using an old Nissen hut left behind by the army and living in its twin. They had built the forecourt and installed the petrol pumps with Lottie and Isobel's father, Douglas Flintock-Smythe. He'd been killed in a crash on the racing circuit at Brooklands, while demonstrating the new brake seal Al's mother had invented. Cassandra, his wife and the girls' mother, never got over his death, in fact, life had not been the same for any of them ever since. But they had won the contract from Stockhead for the brake seals and had created a modest business from it, together with the garage and selling his Dad's vegetables. Now, they had a bungalow instead of the Nissen hut as their home and, although many other businesses had failed in recent years, they had managed to keep going. He wished his parents weren't always so busy and tired though.

The other kids at school teased that he always stank of rubber and he had to listen to a lot of jokes at his expense about 'French Letters'. He'd soon learned to give some quick retorts and shrug off the taunts. In fact, he was known as a bit of a joker and had lots of friends. None of them could match his fondness for the Flintock-Smythe girls, though. They'd grown up together like cousins, so they felt like family. It was great to have them to himself all day, especially with no adults breathing down their necks.

"Come on, I'm starving. It's been ages since breakfast. Let's raid the kitchen. Gran's not here to stop us!" Al led the way into the new bungalow, built by his father with the help of the local builder and the pride and joy of his ambitious mother. It was a pity his grandfather hadn't lived to see it but Agnes, his grandmother, had come to live with them after his death and domestic life had taken quite an upturn. What his mother, Katy Phipps, proprietor of Katherine Wheel Garage and Rubber Factory, didn't know about car engines wasn't worth writing on a postage stamp, but she had no interest in cooking and cleaning.

Al went straight to the larder. "What do you fancy, girls?"

The three girls clustered around him, making him feel like a king dispensing treasure.

"What have you got?"

Al peered inside the big cupboard. The shelves were laden with jars of jams and chutneys, all made by Agnes, and there were slabs of cold marble covered with lace doilies held down with beads at their edges. They looked interesting. He lifted the white covers.

"Ooh, look, there's a ham! And lots of cheese."

"It's so hot today," Lottie said, "let's make a picnic and take it to the river!"

"Oh, yes, that would be so much fun." Lily was always eager for an adventure.

Al looked at Isobel. She was usually the quiet one, but she seemed keen too. "I'd love that."

Al's stomach rumbled. "Okay then, but I need something right now."

Lottie cut thick slices of the fresh bread and Isobel spread them with jam and butter. Lily found a jug of milk, and they each had a glass.

"Oh, that's better!" Al patted his stomach. "Not sure I need a picnic now."

8

Lottie smiled. "You won't say that in a couple of hours, if I know you."

Al laughed. "You know me too well. Come on then, girls, let's get cracking. We're wasting time when we could be out on the river. Me and Dad patched up the old rowing boat last week. We could take her out on the water and see if she's watertight."

"Yes, let's! We could pretend we're sailing the high seas and off to the rubber plantations in Malaya!" Lottie got to work and cut some more bread, thinner this time, and she and Isobel formed a production line with cheese, butter and chutney.

Lily found some clean tea cloths and lined the baskets with them. Al searched deeper into the meat safe at the very back of the larder and came up trumps. "Blimey! Look what I've found! Gran's apple cake. It's tops."

Lily, with her usual resourcefulness, found a wicker basket. Lottie insisted on being the one to pack it. "You have to put the heavy things at the bottom, you see, or the sandwiches will get crushed. Now then, Al, what can you supply for us to drink?"

"Hmm," Al rubbed his forehead. "I know! Gran's lemonade. It's fizzy so we mustn't shake it up on the way or the stoppers might pop."

Another basket was found for the bottles, while Lottie tied the tea cloth over the basket and declared everything was finally ready for the off. "Lead us to our destiny, Captain!"

Al's acknowledged his promotion to leader with a brisk nod. "Ay, ay, crew. Ship ahoy!" They went outside and he gathered up the oars from the shed and gave one to Lottie to carry, putting the other on his shoulder like a soldier with his rifle.

"Forward march, me hearties!" Al picked up a stick he'd whittled the other evening and swished it through the nettles, before leading them through his secret gate to the field beyond his parents' garden.

He closed the gate carefully after them. "Come on, race you to the river!"

Isobel was carrying the bottles. "What about the lemonade?"

"Oh, I expect it'll be alright!" Al had already started running ahead to find out if the boat was moored where he'd left it.

He paused and looked back to check on everyone. Isobel was walking sedately behind the others, holding the stash of lemonade bottles carefully against her chest. Lily, unburdened by a basket, had overtaken her, running as fast as her little legs could go, trying to keep up with him. Both girls looked happy enough. He turned around to face front again, only to see Lottie streaking ahead of him.

"Come on, slowcoach!" she yelled back at him, and ran on again, laughing.

CHAPTER THREE
Isobel

Isobel finally caught up with the others by the little jetty on the riverbank. Even Lily had got there before her and was already ensconced in the little wooden boat with the picnic basket. Isobel didn't mind. She was proud that not one of the lemonade bottles had popped their stoppers under her care.

Lily beckoned her to the dinghy. "Come on, Bella. You've been ages!"

"But look, the lemonade is alright." She held up her basket to show them.

Neither Lottie nor Al noticed. They were too busy fiddling with mooring rope of the boat. She watched them, smiling at how they argued over who was to row.

Al stood, legs apart, hands on hips. "But I'm stronger than you, Lottie."

"No, you're not. I play hockey and tennis and my arms are as strong as any boy's!"

"Bet they're not stronger than mine." Al flexed his arm.

"Alright, we'll have an arm-wrestling contest right now." Lottie stuck out her chin.

Isobel stepped forward. "Do you really have to? It would be much more fun to get going on the river."

Al and Lottie looked back at her. Lottie looked mutinous but Al grinned his lovely big smile. He was so handsome, if you ignored the odd pimple here and there. Isobel didn't mind those. She thought he was gorgeous.

"She's right, you know, Lottie." Al looked back at her sister and lowered his arm.

"Oh, alright then, you can row to start, and I'll take a turn after." Lottie acknowledged defeat by climbing in the little boat. She did it so deftly, it hardly wobbled at all, despite the boat being so much lower than the wooden platform above it. "Shove over, Lily, I'm going to take the tiller."

"But I can do that, Lottie," Lily protested, unwilling to give up the place she usually held when she was in the boat with her Dad and brother, but not letting on that they usually guided her hand on the tiller. She always steered into the bank or the weeds on her own.

"You can do it anytime. Come on, let me have a go." If Isobel was any judge, it was obvious Lottie wasn't going to give way.

Lily sighed and gave up her seat, mumbling, "So unfair."

"You come aboard next, Bella. Give me the bottles first." Al took them from her and stowed them neatly next to the seat in the middle of the boat.

Isobel hesitated on the riverbank. She lacked Lottie's confidence about getting in the dinghy. Now she was close to it, the gap between the wooden jetty and the bottom of the boat looked huge. How had Lottie done it so easily?

Al seemed to sense her fear and quietly gave her his hand. She took it eagerly, glad of his help - and the touch of his fingers. The boat moved fluidly under her as she stepped inside. It was an odd sensation and she didn't like it much. It made her nervous.

Al climbed in last and settled himself in the centre of the boat, between the oars.

"Ready, crew?"

The three girls chorused, "Aye, aye, Captain!"

Al untied the rope that held them secure, pushed an oar against the mossy, wooden bars of the jetty, and they were off.

As they glided aimlessly along the river, Isobel trailed her hand in the green water, letting the fronds of the weeds caress her fingers with their silky bands. She wished she'd brought her watercolours and some paper.

She would love to try and capture the greenness of it all with her paintbrush. The grassy bank with its ratholes; the slithery weeds sliding under the hull of the boat; the white splash of water as the oars dipped in and left a spray of diamonds from their blades. She could drift like this forever, with her favourite people sitting beside her and the unique smell of the river, teeming with life, adding to her relaxation.

Her peace was soon shattered by Lottie insisting it was now her turn with the oars. Oh, why couldn't Lottie just shut up, for once!

CHAPTER FOUR
Lottie

The river opened up into a wider section before them, leaving behind the dense woodland and revealing a shingle bank in the centre. Lottie felt the boat scrape on the sandy pebbles as the river broadened into shallow waters.

"Ship aground!" Al lifted his oars up out of the water.

"Yes, I know!" Lottie ground her teeth and steered the tiller towards the deeper water near the far bank. She could see a channel where the weeds still grew and headed straight for it, hoping the rudder wouldn't get tangled up.

"I'm hungry," Lily said, "When are we going to have our picnic?"

"Honestly, Lily, proper sailors have to go for hours and hours without food on a real voyage." Al dipped his left oar back in the river.

"There's no need to help me, Al, I can manage perfectly well with the tiller." Lottie, annoyed, jerked the tiller too far and the boat tilted.

Lily yelped in alarm. "Ooh, we're going to tip over!"

"Don't worry, Lily. Lottie knows what she's doing." Isobel put her arm around the younger girl.

Lottie grinned at Isobel and felt a bond of kinship with her sister. She moved the tiller arm more smoothly and they glided safely into deeper waters.

"Well done, first mate!" Al nodded at her.

"Who says I'm first mate? I think we should take it in turns to be captain. Whoever's rowing should be in charge." Lottie glared at her friend.

"Can't have two captains." Al resumed rowing.

"Don't see why not." Lottie turned back to look at him.

"Goodness me, you two! Does it really matter? Just keep swopping over, can't you?" It was Isobel's turn to look annoyed now. "And Lily does have a point. We've been on the river for ages. It must be nearly lunchtime and the food will spoil if we don't eat it soon."

The sun was really hot now, it was true. Lottie looked at the baskets, sitting side by side, one covered with the tea cloth she'd tied up so neatly into a white bow, now looking decidedly limp. She'd tried to tuck them under the bench seats of the dinghy, but the handles had got in the way and they were baking in the full sun. Those sandwiches would be all dry and curled up and the lemonade warm.

"Fair enough. Let's look out for a good place to stop. You girls look that side, and Al and I will search this bank."

"Good idea," Al plunged the oars into the water with renewed vigour. "I'm sure there are some beachy bits along here somewhere."

They were all silent as they scanned the riverbank for picnic spots, but none came into view.

"Do you know, I'm getting a bit tired." Al let his oars rest in the rowlocks. "The trouble is, we're going upstream all the time."

"Do you want me to row for a bit?" Lottie had enjoyed steering and would have been happy to carry on. Having taken a turn at the rowing, she now knew what an effort it was, but Al did look fed up.

"Yes, please." Al gave her one of his cheeky grins. The only concession she was likely to get.

They swopped seats and again the boat rocked from side to side, making Lily squeal.

"I want to get out of the boat now. I'd like to be back on land that doesn't move about all the time." Lily grabbed the side of the boat making it tilt even more.

"Sit up, Lily!" Al had only just sat down in the stern himself.

"I do wish the boat would settle again." Isobel looked concerned.

"Honestly how you do fuss, you two." Lottie took up the oars and steadied the boat with them. "See? As long as you know what you're doing, there's no need to panic."

Lily scowled at her. Lottie's arms ached when she began to row again. She was using muscles that weren't used to the motion. She, too, would be glad to stop.

They went around a bend in the river and Lottie tried to build up a rhythm with her rowing action. She was pleased with her speed. Al was right, it was really hard work going against the flow of the river. She couldn't keep it up much longer.

Lottie suspected Isobel had guessed she was tiring from her next remark. "Look, we're not going to find the perfect beach, are we? Let's settle for something that will just have to do. Come on, that bit over there looks good enough to me. We could go on rowing for hours looking for the best spot and still not find it."

"Good idea." Lottie was relieved she didn't have to admit her fatigue in front of the others. She would be so glad to stop rowing.

Al nodded and tacked across the river to the other side to where Isobel was pointing her finger.

"Oh goody," Lily rubbed her tummy. "I'm hungrier than ever. I don't care how long the sailors went without food. I need some now!"

They all laughed. It broke the tension that had been building for the last hour, without Lottie even realising it.

The little dinghy bumped against the bank and Lottie thankfully rested her oars in their rowlocks.

"It's a bit steep." Isobel looked doubtfully at the bank, which was about two feet higher than the bow of the boat.

"I'll get out first, then you, Isobel, and you, Lily. Lottie can stay in the boat and hand the stuff up to us. We'll make a chain gang." Al clutched a clump of grass which promptly came away in his hand. "Oh, that didn't work, did it?"

Lottie thought his smile looked false and that Al was as worried as she now was. "Look, Al, if I row towards that tree root, we can tie up the boat and then try and get out."

Al nodded at her. They were all silent as Lottie gently manoeuvred the boat to a willow tree that grew half in, half out of the water.

Al grabbed the rope coiled on the floor of the boat and leant right out across the bow. "A bit nearer, Lottie. That's it!" Al threw the rope at the tree, but it missed and fell back in the water, sinking in a serpentine coil into the murky depths, where they had churned up the mud from the bottom.

Lottie stuck an oar into the riverbed, trying to anchor the boat. The mud beneath the water was sludgy and loose and wouldn't grip the wood. "I can't hold it much longer, Al!"

Al was pulling up the rope with both hands.

Isobel gave a hollow laugh. "Looks like you're fishing, Al. We'll have to make a fire and cook it, if you catch something."

None of the others laughed back but looked anxiously as Al threw the rope a second time. It slithered back into the river, heavy and saturated.

"I'll have to get out." Al looked at Lottie. "How deep is it, do you reckon?"

"Only about two feet, I should think, but you'll get soaked. Maybe we should go on for a bit, find an easier place."

"But I'm hungry." Lily piped up again.

"No, it's okay. I can do it." Al rolled his shorts up as high as they would go and took off his canvas shoes.

Isobel looked worried. "You might cut your feet on a stone, like that, Al."

Lottie scoffed. "Judging by the mud I can feel with my oar, he's more likely to get sucked under."

Lily squealed. "Oh, Al, don't do it!"

Al laughed unconvincingly. "Don't be silly, Lily. I'll be fine." He lowered himself into the water. "Ugh, yuck. It's really slimy."

Al waded over to the tree and easily slung the rope around its trunk. He tied it off and then clambered up, using the roots as hand holds, on to the grassy bank. "Easy peasy!"

Lottie was more relieved than she let on to the others. "Well done, Al. Come on Lily and Bella, let's unload our grub."

Al stood on the bank, his naked feet planted firmly on the grass and held out his hands to Isobel. She stood up, looking very nervous but determined, and reached out to him. "Come on, Bella." Al's voice softened. "One big stride and you're on dry land. I'll take your weight. You can do it."

Compressing her lips, Isobel reached out and held both Al's hands. Lottie knew a moment of real fear as he tipped forward momentarily as Isobel's slender body, light though it was, drew him towards the river. For an instant, it looked like they would both fall in, but Al leaned back and pulled Isobel into his arms. They collapsed on the grass in a heap.

"Phew! Thank goodness you're alright." Lottie let out her breath. "Come on, Lily, you next."

"Ooh, I'm not sure I can do it." Lily looked really scared.

"Of course, you can. I'll be behind you and you've got both Bella and Al to catch you." Lottie helped the younger girl stand up. The boat lurched violently.

"I don't like it!" Lily wailed.

"Well, it's just as well you'll soon be a landlubber then." Al stood up and reached out his hands.

"Come on, do it quickly, before you think about it." Lottie braced herself with her legs wide apart and held Lily in front of her. "Here she comes, Al."

Lily leant forward and the boat veered away from the bank. Lily screamed as she stepped out, but Al caught her in the nick of time and Isobel grabbed her other hand. With their combined strength they hauled her up the bank.

Al laughed once she was safely landed. "Blimey, Lily, you'll have to go for a swim later. You're plastered in mud!" His laughter was infectious, and everyone but Lily joined in.

Lily pouted. "You know I can't swim, Al."

Lottie relaxed at last. She knew she could get out and didn't care if she fell in or not. The other two girls were such sissies. She started handing up the baskets. The others formed a chain and they soon had the baskets unloaded.

"We should have brought a rug to sit on." Isobel was busy setting out the food.

"Nonsense. Pirates don't have such luxuries." Al was already munching on a sandwich and talked through his mouthful of cheese and bread.

Suddenly, one of the lemonade bottles made a loud bang, like a gun going off. They all jumped, and Al nearly choked on his food.

"Oh no! The lemonade is fizzing. It must have got hot in the boat." Isobel frowned.

"I know, let's dangle it in the river to cool off. I read somewhere about explorers doing that." Lottie jumped up and carried a bottle to the riverside. "Now, what can I ty it with? We need some string to go around its neck."

"Use my shoelace." Al still hadn't put his shoes back on.

Lottie took the shoe, unlaced it and tied the string around the neck of the bottle and the other end around the tree root. "There! It's perfect. Let's do another one."

There were only three bottles left as the one that had popped its stopper had spent its load. Lottie unlaced one of her own shoes and hooked the other two bottles around the willow tree root with the first. The bottles bobbed up and down in the water, half hidden by the willow fronds, gracefully dangling down over them.

Satisfied, she went back to the group. "They will be lovely and cold in half an hour and we can wash our lunch down with cool drinks."

Isobel handed her a sandwich. "Your prize, Miss Cleverclogs."

Lottie took a bite. It was delicious, although a little warm. "Don't mind if I do."

CHAPTER FIVE
Al

Now his stomach was full, Al felt a little drowsy. A blue-bottle fly landed on the leftovers of the picnic, scattered on the tea towels that lay in a heap amongst them. He lay back, listening to its drone. His eyelids were heavy and unwilling to remain open. Within minutes, he was asleep and dreaming of sailing boats on wide, tumbling seas, his hands on the helm, his eyes scanning the horizon for pirate ships.

A scream jarred him awake.

"Get off me, get off me, you horrid thing." Al opened his eyes to see Lily flailing her arms about wildly.

"What's the matter?" Al mumbled the words.

"It's only a wasp, Lily, calm down." Lottie looked scornful.

But Lily was up on her feet with the wasp in hot pursuit. "It won't leave me alone!"

Isobel got up, grabbed a tea towel and flapped it at the insect.

"Oh no, there's a whole nest of them!" Isobel looked alarmed now and Al woke right up.

"Right, we'd better abandon the rest of the food, there's not much left anyway except Gran's cake."

"But look at it, Al." Isobel pointed at the cake, as yet uncut, but now swarming with wasps. He could barely see the sponge underneath the buzzing creatures.

"It's the sugar." Lottie sighed. "I was so looking forward to a piece of that."

"Back to the boat, girls." Al scooped up the remaining tea towel and shook the crumbs off it. His shoes had lain just next to the cake and the wasps hummed more angrily as he approached them. He had to snatch them away from the swarm with only an inch to spare, flapping the tea cloth at them through the operation.

21

"Oh, be careful, Al! You'll make them angry like that." Isobel looked alarmed. "What do you use for a wasp sting? Vinegar, isn't it?"

Al crammed his lace-less shoes back on his feet, stuffing his socks in the pocket of his shorts. His feet slopped about in the loose canvas shoes. He'd have a job keeping them on in the boat.

"Well, surprisingly, I don't happen to have any with me." Lottie frowned at Al, hopping about with one shoe on. "I hope you've checked there isn't a wasp inside your socks."

Al, more frightened than he cared to admit, threw the socks away in horror. "Eek! I'll just leave them here. Come on, get in the boat."

The girls hurried to the riverbank and he quickly joined them, clawing his toes to keep his shoes on. "Come on, get in. Once we're away from the food, they'll leave us alone. They want the sugar in the cake, not us."

"I'll get in first." Lottie stepped neatly into centre of the boat. "You next, Lily." She held out her arms to the little girl, who jumped into them and clung to her for a moment. "Sit down carefully in the stern."

Lily did as she was told.

"Come on, Isobel. You next." Al spoke softly in her ear. He knew she was terrified of falling in the water and looking a fool in front of her older sister. "You can do it," he added in a whisper only she could hear.

Isobel gave him a secret smile of gratitude. Her eyes, a lovely, deep cornflower blue, silently told him she understood. He held her hand in a firm grip and then put his arms around her waist, holding her steady. She trembled slightly under his touch. How brave she was, being so frightened but not showing it to anyone.

"Ready?" Al still spoke in a low whisper.

Isobel nodded.

"One, two, three – go!" Al gave her the gentlest of pushes and Isobel jumped into her sister's arms.

"Honestly, Bella, there's nothing to it, is there?" Lottie quickly let go of her sister and held her hand out to Al.

He grabbed it and quickly boarded the little dinghy. "All aboard! Now then, crew, let's get away from these confounded pests."

"I'll row." Lottie had already taken up position on the middle bench. "And we'll go back downstream and let the river do the work."

"Good idea," Al spoke with feeling. His arms still ached from this morning's hard work.

CHAPTER SIX
Isobel

Isobel leant her back against the wooden bench seat and allowed herself to relax. She hated wasps, having been stung by one when she was little. It had hurt. Thank goodness no-one had got stung this time. It was a pity about the cake, though. She'd looked forward to a bit of that, too.

She wasn't really hungry, though. Agnes's bread was delicious and the cheese and chutney no less so. Isobel didn't have a big appetite anyway, not like Lottie, or Al, for that matter.

She looked down at Lily, sitting next to her in the bow of the little rowing boat. Lily's head was nodding towards her shoulder, so she put her arm around the younger girl and tucked her up close against her body. Lily's head drooped and her eyes closed. She could tell from her steady breathing that the little girl had quickly fallen asleep.

Al was rowing and Lottie steering the boat. For once, they weren't arguing but seemed content to sit in companionable silence together as the current bore them back to their starting point. Isobel's own eyes started to become heavy. She let her head drop on to Lily's and gave up fighting the sleepy feeling.

She had a raging thirst when she woke up. Lily was still asleep, and Al had let his oars rest in their rowlocks. His head was bowed, and his chin lay on his chest. Lottie had stretched out in the stern and had lain her head against the pile of discarded jumpers piled on top of the baskets. They were both dozing too! Isobel smiled at her sister and their friend, both usually so energetic, far more than she was. She always felt as if she wasn't good enough in their company, much as she loved them. She knew a moment of satisfaction on seeing that they too had succumbed to the humid warm weather and the after-effects of Agnes's good food.

Isobel ignored her thirst; she didn't want to disturb the others. She looked around at the riverbanks on either side of the floating boat, alarmed she could not recognise any landmarks, but then, she told herself, she didn't know the river that well. She trailed her fingers in the silky water again, loving its cool feel against her sweaty palm and gazing at the ripples made by the bow of the boat as it glided along its surface. A shoal of little fishes swam past, their silver backs glinting in the sun's rays through the watery world below.

The riverbanks seemed to be stretching further away all the time. Isobel thought idly it must be widening out, but she couldn't remember being on this section before. She licked her dry lips. Where was that lemonade? Then she remembered. Oh no! they'd left it behind, tied to the willow tree root in the river water. Isobel looked back down at the river. The green water was full of bugs and weeds, she didn't fancy drinking that. There was nothing else for it, she'd have to wake up the others.

"Wakey, wakey, everyone!" Isobel spoke softly, in her normal voice, and it had no effect. She said it again, much louder this time.

"Wazzat?" Al turned around. "Ow, my neck is stiff."

Lottie jerked her head up. "Hmm? Where are we?"

Lily lifted her head up from Isobel's lap, to where it had gradually slipped down during her nap. She sat up and rubbed her eyes. "I'm thirsty."

"Anyone know where we are?" Isobel, feeling more awake than the others, was keen to know the answer.

Al raked his hand through his chestnut curls and looked about. "River's wider here."

Lottie nodded. She'd woken right up straight away and still hadn't a hair out of place. Isobel could never fathom how she did that. Lottie woke up every morning with her hairpins in order.

"Al, do you think we've drifted past the mooring below your garden?"

Al scratched his head. "Dunno. Don't recognise this spot. How long have we been asleep?"

Lottie looked at her watch. She'd won it at school for a French oral exam. Isobel sighed. Lottie was so *good* at everything.

"Goodness! We've been dozing for an hour! Did your Grandmother put a sleeping potion in that loaf of bread?"

Al bridled at this. "Don't blame my Gran for your snoozing."

Isobel tried to keep the peace. It never lasted long enough for her. "Now then, you two. Let's concentrate on where we are, not waste time arguing. Don't suppose you have a map, do you, skipper?"

Al's scowl disappeared. "Afraid not. We could have drifted a long way past my place, I'm just not sure. I wish I'd left a note to say where we were going."

Lottie frowned. "You're right. I completely forgot to do that. But we'll be back before tea and no-one will be any the wiser. Your mum told us to keep out of her hair and ours is off gallivanting in London. Now, let's think. We need some landmarks. It's impossible to tell with all the willow trees either side. Let's go a bit further and see if there's an opening so we can tell where we are."

"Won't we be further away from Al's house though, assuming we've already past it?" Isobel didn't often challenge her sister, but this seemed a mad idea.

"Don't be silly, Bella. We rowed for hours and hours this morning. I should know!" Lottie, as usual, ignored her suggestion.

Isobel looked at Al, but he just looked worried and remained silent, scanning the riverbanks.

"I'm so thirsty." Lily smacked her lips, which looked very dry. "Can we have the lemonade now?"

Isobel squeezed her arm. "Sorry, Lily, but we forgot them in our hurry to get away from the wasps. The bottles are still tied up to that willow tree in the water."

Lily's chin started to tremble. "I want to go home."

Al looked at his little sister. "Come on, now, Lily. Brace up. I know, let's pretend we're pirates and looking for treasure. We'll sing some shanties, shall we?" Al broke into song.

> *"What shall we do with the drunken sailor,*
> *What shall we do with the drunken sailor,*
> *What shall we do with the drunken sailor?*
> *Early in the morning."*

Isobel joined in, just to cheer Lily up but Lottie scowled. "How can the sailor get drunk if there's no drink for him?"

"And it's not the morning, it's the afternoon." Lily wriggled away from Isobel's protecting arm. She looked hot and tired.

"Look, let's get around this bend and see if we can tell where we are, hey?" Al picked up his oars and began to row. Come on, Lily, you think of a song this time."

Lily had a good voice, stronger than her small frame promised and she loved to sing. She stopped sulking and smiled as she sang:

> *"Row, row, row the boat, gently down the stream,*
> *Merrily, merrily, merrily, merrily,*
> *Life is but a dream."*

Al laughed and the others joined in. "Great choice, Lily!"

27

Lottie smiled too. "Let's sing it in the round, one after the other."

Isobel shook her head. "Oh, Lottie, you always have to make things complicated." But she joined in with the others. It was fun to keep the song going, one after the other. Isobel stopped thinking about her thirst and they sped along the river much faster as they sang at the tops of their voices.

CHAPTER SEVEN
Lottie

Lottie forgot all about the steering while she focussed on her round of singing. When the others dried up in fits of laughter, she was the only one left. She sang the whole verse to the end in triumph. The others clapped, Al letting his oars fall back into the rowlocks with a clunk. As their blades dug into the water, the boat juddered and veered off course.

Lottie grabbed the tiller and pulled it back to centre. She looked around. The river was narrowing again, making the flow faster and the water deeper as it cut a channel between its steep banks. Little waves formed on the previously smooth surface of the river as it gathered pace.

"Are we nearly home now?" Lily looked to her older brother. She looked confident of his answer, but Lottie could see that Al was less so.

"Um, probably. What do you think, Lottie?"

Lottie looked up at the sky, desperately seeking some sort of landmark. If they had passed the garage by and were nearing the village of Lower Cheadle, surely, they'd see the church spire?

Instead, she glimpsed the roof of her own home, Cheadle Manor, whose three gables were so familiar and dear to her. "Look! It's our house! We've already gone past the village without even noticing!"

The other three children whirled their heads around to where her finger pointed, jabbing at the sky.

"So, we're miles away from the garage." Al looked a bit panicky.

Isobel looked at Lottie. "That means we're approaching our lake, doesn't it?"

Lottie nodded. "Yes, we'd better get moored up before we reach the weir."

Al started rowing like mad. "I'd forgotten about the weir. I didn't think we were anywhere near it. We're much farther along than I thought. I'll turn the boat."

Lily was silent. She hunched up next to Isobel who put her arm back around the younger girl.

"Where can we stop, Al?" Lottie had kept to the middle of the river, where it was deepest. She looked at each bank in turn, but she could see no easy mooring place amongst the willow trees that covered them right down to the water's edge. Al's attempt to turn the boat around back upstream had failed dismally. There was no denying it - the river had them in its grip and was propelling them downstream at an ever-increasing speed.

"I don't know, Lottie. Never been on this stretch of the river in my life before." Al dug the oars in against the current again but only succeeded in jarring the dinghy and making them grip its sides.

"Really? I've never been on a boat round here either, but I think the weir must be ages away. I'll go closer to the bank on the other side and then we'll be able to see round the next bend. Maybe we'll find something to moor against." Lottie steered to the far side of the river and craned her neck to look beyond to see what lay ahead.

As soon as they emerged from the sharp curve, limestone walls reared up on either side of them and the river shrank into a narrow sluice of much deeper water.

Lily screamed. "What's that noise? Is it thunder?"

"It's the weir!" Isobel clutched Lily with one hand and the side of the little wooden dinghy with the other.

"Brace yourselves, my hearties." Al gave a crooked smile.

"Hold on tight!" Lottie yelled as loud as she could over the crashing roar of the water. She braced her legs against Al's bench in front of her, her foot slipping in the shoe without laces, and gripped the sides of the boat, letting the tiller run free. The river ahead cascaded in a white rush between the high walls of limestone covered in green moss, too slippery to give a hand hold. All of a sudden, they had joined the racing water. All Lottie could hear was its boom as it shot forward in a green shimmering chute before falling and breaking up into a million white spheres of foam. The image was fleeting; she had only seconds to register the impression before the little boat launched itself into the air above the waterfall, momentarily suspended in dry air above the cacophony.

They were all screaming now, even Lottie. She knew real terror in those moments, then the dinghy crashed down into the frothing waves, bouncing violently from side to side. Lottie couldn't think at all then as she was thrown out into the white spume and dragged down under the bubbles, which forced their way down her throat, blocking her airways. Her loose shoe lifted off her foot and floated away. Something banged against her head. She shut her eyes, stunned by its impact. All she could taste was river water; all she could feel was its cold pressure pushing her down, buffeting her as the water cascaded above her.

She couldn't move her arms and legs. They wouldn't respond, they were too heavy. She couldn't think above the roaring noise in her ears as the churning water rushed in, squeezing her brain so it wouldn't work either.

She wanted to give up struggling, let the water swallow her up, go with its flow, do whatever it wanted to do with her. The river was bigger than she was; she couldn't fight it. Down, down, down, into the depths she sank, listless, overwhelmed by the weight of the water drumming on to her head. She closed her eyes in defeat.

Then, all by itself, her body tipped sideways. She'd been vertical, more or less, submerging into the waterfall feet first. Now, she was on her side, and, involuntarily, her feet started kicking, fighting back. Then her arms joined in. Without conscious thought, Lottie instinctively began to swim. She opened her eyes, seeing only murky, bubbly water around her, nothing above. And yet, wasn't that a glimmer of sunlight? She forced her legs to move in frog-like movements towards that life-giving sun, beckoning to her through the green river. Lottie swung her arms against its watery force, defying its greedy suck, pushing against the fluid resistance until she gained the surface, well away from the sluice gate and into the calm waters of the lake belonging to her own home, Cheadle Manor.

All this was registered in seconds. Lottie gasped for air, snatching at the oxygen. Her lungs felt like they might burst. She coughed out water, took in more air. When the oxygen reached her brain, she immediately looked around for the others. Where were they? Where was Al? Isobel? Little Lily? Oh, God! Where were they? Had they stayed in the boat? Could that be possible?

As more air reached her lungs, her legs worked better and she wiped the hair from her eyes, casting about in circles. There was the boat, capsized and drifting away. Who knew where the oars were! Was anyone trapped underneath its hull?

"Al?" Her voice was a croak and barely a whisper. She turned around, frantic to find the others.

Then she saw Lily. Her little head was bobbing in and out of the water, her hands up in the air and then sinking below the water line. She wasn't too far away. Could Lottie reach her before she drowned?

Lottie put her head down into her best crawl position. She powered her way towards Lily – or to where she had been. She caught the remnants of a ripple in the same place and dived down. Lily was sinking fast below the water. Lottie dived deeper and swam with all her strength towards the drowning girl. With the last of her strength, she grabbed Lily around the waist and held her to her chest. The little girl was limp in her arms and unconscious, and a stream of bubbles rose up from her open mouth to join the air so far above them. It made her feel much heavier than she really was. Lottie kicked her legs as hard as she could. For a moment, she didn't think she could stay afloat with Lily's added weight. She looked up to the surface. Again, that burning sun invited her to make one last effort.

She used one of her hands to power a push upwards, holding on to Lily with the other, rather than both. Her arm ached. Lily was a deadweight, but with the extra impetus of her arm thrashing at the water, that golden globe shimmering through the lake drew her upwards until she was again gasping for air above its treacherous surface.

She snatched again at the oxygen it provided. Her ribs ached as she forced them to expand, drawing down the air into the waiting chambers of her empty lungs. Lottie flicked her wet hair out of her eyes and looked at Lily, so limp in her tired arms.

"Lily? Lily? Wake up! Oh, God, Lily!" Lottie was crying now, adding warm tears to the cool lake water. She shook her friend. It was so frightening the way Lily was so white, as white as the flower she was named after, the flower that symbolised death.

"Lily!" Lottie screamed the name now and shook her again. Nothing.

"Oh, God!" Lottie looked around her. Where were the others? She couldn't turn a full circle, with Lily's weight dragging at her.

"Lily!" Lottie suddenly remembered something the sports mistress had taught her. If someone's lungs were full of water, turn them over and squeeze their tummies to eject it. Could she do it while swimming? Time was of the essence. She must try.

Kicking madly with her legs to stop them sinking down into the depths again, Lottie took the risk of using both her arms to turn her burden so that Lily's faced away from her. Treading water with weary legs, Lottie wrapped both arms around Lily's middle and drew them towards herself, pressing flat palms against Lily's belly.

She was alarmed at the gargling sound that emanated from the little girl. She couldn't see her face now. Was it under water? Lottie couldn't take her weight much longer; the water was dangerously close to her own nose and mouth as she struggled. Lily's abdomen lurched under her hands and it sounded like she was being sick. Lottie twizzled Lily back around to face her again.

"Lily! Lily! Oh, come back to me, Lily!" Lottie squeezed the girl's stomach again and more water spurted out of Lily's mouth. Then, to Lottie's utter relief, Lily took a breath.

Lottie gasped. "Oh, thank God!"

Lily opened her eyes. They were deep blue, like her mother's. She blinked. Her springy black curls lay flat against her wet head. She was as white as her name.

Lottie couldn't relax, not even now her legs and arms were screaming in pain. "Lily. We're in the lake at Cheadle Manor. You're going to have to swim. Alright?"

Lily shook her head. "Can't."

"What do you mean, you can't?"

"Swim. Can't."

Lottie knew real despair at that moment. She must think. Think!

She looked around, searching for refuge. The lake immediately spread out after the sluice gate, so its banks were much too far away for her to reach, but there was a little island for ducks in the middle of the lake. Of course! The island! Lottie turned a half circle. There it was! It was much nearer than the edges of the lake, but it still looked miles away - impossibly far away.

34

Lottie faced her friend, still spluttering and choking in her arms.

"Lily. Listen to me. I know you can't swim but you can kick your legs while I hold you. See that little island there?" Lottie pointed to it, but Lily was too faint to look. "Never mind if you can't see it. All you've got to do is trust me. Can you do that, Lily?"

Lily gave a weak nod.

"Good. Now, don't panic but I'm going to lift your legs a bit higher, so you are flatter in the water, as if you were swimming. It will feel strange at first, but you mustn't be frightened. The water will take your weight, even though it doesn't feel like it. Ready?"

Lily, barely conscious, nodded fractionally. It would have to do.

"Just trust me, Lily, that's your job; that's all you have to do. Trust me. Keep your mouth closed tight and breathe through your nose."

Lottie put one arm under Lily's legs and lifted them parallel with the surface water.

Lily's eyes opened wide in fear.

"Remember not to panic, Lily. I've got you. You're safe. Now, hold on to me with your arm, like this." Lottie grabbed Lily's hand and placed it on the belt of her shorts, making sure Lily had a firm hold. "Good girl. You're doing brilliantly. Now, Lily. You must help me with your other arm. I know you're tired but so am I and we've got to do this together. I want you to wave your arm in the water, sort of through it, if you like. Pretend it's a windmill and push the water behind you, like a fish does with its tail." Lottie could barely believe her luck when Lily complied. A sob caught in her throat. She steeled herself not to cry again. She couldn't afford the spare energy.

"Oh, well done, darling!" Lottie placed her other arm around Lily's tiny waist and gripped it firmly. "Now, let's go! We'll have an arm each to push us along and now we must kick as hard as we can with our legs and feet. Can you do that?"

Instantly, Lily felt lighter as she moved her legs. They started to progress in the water towards the little island. At least there was no current against them this time, as in the river. The pain in Lottie's limbs eased as Lily joined in, with the water supporting her rather than pulling her down. Once or twice Lily gagged as a little wavelet, propelled by their motion, slopped into her mouth. She'd opened it straight away as she panted with the effort of trying to swim.

Each time, Lottie encouraged her, but by the time they reached the island, she barely had enough strength to speak at all. When her bare foot touched the gravelly bed of the lake, she was completely exhausted and knew she couldn't have swum another yard.

"We've made it, Lily!" Lottie gasped out the words.

The feel of the solid ground under her was the most wonderful thing she'd ever experienced. Soon, Lily touched base too and gave her a feeble smile from her wan face. They scrambled up the short beach and collapsed on to the shingle.

Ducks flapped up in the air in alarm at their appearance, quacking noisily. It was the last thing Lottie heard before she passed out.

CHAPTER EIGHT
Al

Al dragged Isobel up the shingly beach. Hand in hand, they threw themselves against the blessed ground. Completely short of breath and very dizzy, he couldn't utter a word.

He looked at Isobel. She looked a bit blue around the mouth and was shivering violently. He shuffled his exhausted body next to hers and pulled her against his chest. Isobel leant into him. He could feel her heart hammering away next to his. He put his arms around her and held her tight. Slowly, he leaned back onto the wet ground and let her lay across him. Al closed his eyes, not caring about her weight on top of him, and let go into a profound, irresistible sleep.

When he awoke, Isobel still lay on top of him but now the pressure was too much for his weary body. Gently, he shook her, and she rose to a sitting position. She looked confused for a moment. He wasn't too sure what had happened either, but he was glad, very glad, Isobel was with him.

Isobel blinked a couple of times and rubbed her eyes. "Where are we?"

Al sat up and looked around. The sun had sunk lower in the sky. They must have been asleep for a while. He willed his brain to function again, but his mind was dull and sluggish.

"I don't know, but at least we are on dry land."

"The boat?"

"Capsized."

"Where is it?"

"No idea." He scanned the lake for the remains of the boat.

"I think we're on the island in the lake where the ducks live."

"Are we?"

Isobel nodded. "Yes, I'm sure of it."

"But where are the others? We don't even know if they made it."

Isobel looked aghast. "Oh, God! Surely they did?"

Al tried to stem his own escalating fear. "Maybe Lottie swam to the edge of the lake and has gone for help?"

"But what about Lily?"

"Oh, Bella! She can't swim!" Galvanised, Al ran to the edge of the water. "I must go back in and find her!"

"But Al, she could be anywhere. You'd never find her! What if Lottie rescued her? Maybe they're halfway to the manor by now?"

"But what if not? Oh, Bella. She could be drowned; my little sister! What can I do?"

Isobel stood up. She'd stopped shivering. "We'll search the island first. That's what we'll do. If Lily is still on the water, we'll still see her if we walk all the way round it. It's only small. We can see every bit of the lake that way. You never know, Lily may have clung to the boat or an oar, or something."

"Yes, yes!" Al started running. He felt completely panicked at the thought of Lily drowning and it would be all his fault. His parents would never forgive him. Agnes would never forgive him. He'd never forgive himself.

They were halfway around the circumference of the islet when he saw them.

"Lily!" Al sprinted towards Lottie and Lily, sprawled together in a heap on the beach, their feet still caressed by the tiny waves washed up by the lake.

"Oh, Bella! They're not moving!"

Isobel joined him and they stared down at the two girls. "Turn them over, Al." Isobel's voice was grave.

Al knelt down. Lily was lying on top of Lottie, who was on her back against the gravel. As he turned

Lily's small body over, a gush of water spewed from her slack mouth. Instinct made him slap her back between her shoulder blades. His heart lifted when Lily coughed and then spluttered out yet more of that hateful river.

"Lily!" Isobel knelt next to him.

Lily opened her eyes. "Al? Bella?"

Al exhaled. "Oh, thank God. You're alive, Lily." He held her to him so tightly, she murmured complaint. He kissed her face all over. "Thank God, thank God."

Isobel pressed a sympathetic hand to his shoulder and got up. He turned to see her go to her sister. She touched Lottie's neck and chest and her face, set so grimly for one so pretty, relaxed. She turned tear-filled eyes to Al and nodded. "She's alive too."

"Come on. Let's take them up and away from the water's edge." Al scooped up his sister and carried her to a group of trees where the sunlight cast long, lingering rays of amber.

He came back to Lottie and Isobel. "Best if she wakes up and helps. I haven't the strength to carry her and neither have you."

Isobel nodded quietly. Together, they put an arm each around Lottie's back and raised her upright to a sitting position. Al didn't like the way Lottie's head lolled backwards.

"We must rouse her, Bella. She might have water in her lungs too."

"I agree." Isobel shook her sister's shoulder roughly. "Lottie. You must wake up. You're on dry land. You've made it, darling. Come on, wake up."

Lottie groaned and her head plopped forward.

Al looked at Isobel. "She's as limp as a rag doll. She can't walk. We'll have to frogmarch her away from the water."

As one, they looped their arms around Lottie's flaccid body and dragged her up the small beach to where

39

Lily sat against the tree trunk. When they moved her, Lottie, too, coughed up some fluid and she moaned.

They propped Lottie up against the next tree trunk and flopped back down next to their sisters. Al grabbed Isobel's hand. "We're all alive, Bella, we're alive."

A sob escaped him; he couldn't stop it. To think he might have killed them all with his mad adventure. His sister, his best friends; he couldn't bear it. More sobs erupted through his body and he could not keep them down. His frame shook with them. Isobel came to him then and put her arms around him. He clung to her and cried unashamedly into her embrace.

CHAPTER NINE
Isobel

Isobel felt strangely comforted by Al's complete breakdown in her arms. He trusted her. That meant a lot. Soon, he regained control of himself and drew away, but not too far away. They sat, shoulder to shoulder, and watched as the sunlight finally faded and gave way to a glimmering twilight. The sun's last rays were reflected in the water surrounding them. It mirrored the spectacle of red, orange and purple colours vying for dominance in the vast sky.

As the light dimmed, little creatures stirred in the undergrowth, making Isobel very uneasy. She seemed to be the only one awake and that made her uneasier still. Something long and thin slithered past her and, involuntarily, she screamed.

"Ah! A snake!" Isobel stuffed her hand in her mouth to stop her own noise, but it was too late. Al and Lottie, startled by the sound, jerked awake. Isobel wasn't sorry to have their company again. She stood up, ready to run away from the snake but it had already rustled away into the bushes and trees behind them.

She shook with fear. She hated anything reptilian. They terrified her.

"What's up, Bella?" Al stood up and held her arms, searching her face with his warm, brown eyes.

"Snake." Isobel pointed to where the creature had slithered away.

Al looked around. "Can't see anything. It must have gone. They are shy creatures."

"What are?" Lottie had opened her eyes and drew her hands across them.

Al answered. "Snakes. Bella's seen one."

"Hello, Lottie, good to have you back." Isobel went to her sister and hugged her.

Lottie weakly hugged her back. Even in the half-light, Isobel could see how grey her skin was, how exhausted her eyes.

But Lottie being Lottie, once roused, she immediately pursued the answer to her question. "You've seen a snake? What type? Was it an adder? Was it aggressive? What markings did it have?"

Isobel laughed. "Oh, Lottie! I don't know. I couldn't see it that well and even if I had, I wouldn't be able to identify it, especially now it's getting dark."

"Yes, it is getting dark. Al? I think we should light a fire. Don't we bash two stones together or something?" Lottie was standing now, looking more her normal self.

Al scratched his head. "We did it in Scouts. Now, let me think. I'm not sure exactly, I think we do need two stones, one bigger than the other to act as an anvil. Then we keep striking them against each other until we make a spark, or something like that."

Lottie nodded her head decisively. "Good. So, we need something dry and small to make it catch?"

Al nodded back. "That's right. Bella, see what you can collect – anything tinder-dry dry and sort of thready, if you know what I mean?"

Isobel remembered the terrifying snake. "But, what about the snake? Won't we disturb it and risk getting bitten?"

Lottie shook her head. "Most snakes will run away at the slightest noise and anyway, my biology teacher said they're active in the daylight – they need the sun to warm up."

"If you're sure?" Isobel looked at the leaves on the woodland floor, wondering what might be lurking underneath.

Lottie immediately began to root about in the undergrowth, looking completely unperturbed and very determined.

Al turned to Isobel. "Tell you what, Bella. You search for the stones instead. Remember, one must be flattish and the other more angular. Can you do that? There's lots by the shoreline."

Isobel breathed more freely. "Of course, I can. What about Lily? Do you think she's alright? We ought to check on her."

They both went to Lily, who was fast asleep. Isobel bent down over her and felt her pulse. It seemed normal and regular. She put her hand flat against Lily's heart and smiled when she felt its steady beat. Lily was a bit cold, but there were no covers they could put over her. The sooner they lit a fire, the better.

Satisfied, she stood up. "She's fine. I'll look for the stones."

"Try and get dry ones, above the waterline." Al had already joined Lottie searching the undergrowth for twigs and dry leaves.

Isobel went towards the water, leaving behind the enclosing cover of the trees. The lake came into full view. She looked across its shimmering surface. Now she was a bit further round the little island, Cheadle Manor was just visible in the distance, hugging the horizon. All the lights in its many windows were blazing out. Of course! None of the grown-ups knew where they were! Granny would be frantic. Katy Phipps too. Maybe they were out searching for them? Surely, someone from the garage would have noticed that their boat was missing? But if not, why would they look for them by the river? It would be like looking for a needle in a haystack for the grown-ups if they didn't realise that.

"You know, a fire is just what we need." Isobel shouted to the others in the woods. "And not just to warm up and see off the wildlife. Look at our house over there."

Lottie and Al turned came to join her at her new vantage point. They stared across the water.

43

Isobel pointed to the manor. "See all the lights? Everyone must be looking for us. Come on, the sooner we have flames going, the sooner they'll find us!" Isobel turned back to her hunt, even more motivated now into finding the perfect flintstones.

Lottie looked at her, then back at their home. "You're right, Bella! We must make sure we light the fire facing the house."

Al grinned. "It's going to be alright, girls. We'll light a blaze you can see for miles and miles!"

Isobel wasn't sure that would be necessary, and could be quite dangerous, but her heart lifted at the thought of rescue, although she dreaded what Granny would say.

She cast about just above the rippling tiny waves of the lake in the gloaming light. She found a striking stone quite easily. It was long and weapon-like, easy to hold. A big flat stone was harder to find but eventually, before the light disappeared completely, she found one. It was about six inches in diameter, smooth and flat.

"Found it!" Isobel crowed to the others.

"Good!" Al dropped his load of twigs on to a pile of thin sticks between them. "Let's see what you've found." He smiled at Isobel. "Bella, they are perfect!"

Isobel was pleased. She placed the flat stone down on the ground and gave Al the long one. "You do it, Al."

Lottie joined them. "Now, we must make sure we face the house so they can see the flames. Here, this looks about right. I've found some dry lichen which I think might catch the spark and here's some dry grass I pinched from a bird's nest."

"But the poor birds?" Isobel couldn't steal from a nest, not even though her life depended on it.

"Oh, don't worry, Bella," Lottie said. "The chicks are long gone at this time of year. Summer's almost over, that's why it's getting dark earlier."

"You're a genius, Lottie." Al took the dry debris of the nest. "This is exactly the sort of thing we were told to hunt for at Scouts."

Isobel watched as Al carefully laid some of the dry grass on the flintstone and started to strike the stones together. It looked like hard work. Al repeated the strike at least a hundred times, it seemed to Isobel, although she was far too tired to count.

"Got to rest." Al looked downcast.

"I'll have a go." Lottie took the long stone from him and hit it against the resting one. "Gosh, it's really hot on the tip, Al. I think you were nearly there."

Isobel willed the spark to come. It was fully dark now and her legs were getting eaten alive by midges. She slapped her legs. "Get off!"

Lily, still behind them near the trees, stirred at the sound. Isobel went over to the little girl and felt her arms. They were very cold. She knew she must get her to wake up and move around before she got completely chilled.

"Come on, Lily. Wakey, wakey."

Lily moaned. She was so pale. Isobel felt guilty. They shouldn't have left her so long on her own. She put her arms around Lily's back and made her more upright. Isobel stroked and tapped Lily's face and rubbed her feet. Gradually, painfully slowly, Lily started to twitch her limbs. Isobel was really worried now. She'd read about people dying of cold.

"Lily! Time to get up, dear." Isobel rubbed Lily's thighs now and moved her arms up and down in a see-saw motion.

"Leave me 'lone. Wanna sleep."

Al called across. "Is she alright?"

Isobel shook her head. "I think she's really chilled. Get that fire going, you two!"

She turned back to the little girl. "Come on, Lily, darling. Let's move those legs of yours." She pumped

Lily's legs up and down. Lily stirred properly at this imposition and pushed Isobel weakly away.

Cheered by her grumpy resistance, Isobel pulled the little girl upright to a standing position. "That's it, good girl! You can do it."

Lily flopped against her. It was obvious her legs wouldn't take her own weight, so Isobel put her arms under Lily's armpits and virtually dragged her to the others.

Al looked exhausted. "It's just not going to work. Now I come to think of it, we used flint and steel at scouts, not stone against stone. How stupid of me not to remember." He opened the flap of the inner pocket of his shorts. "Look! I've still got my penknife. Thank goodness this pocket is buttoned up on my shorts and it didn't fall out in the water. Lottie, let's go and look for some proper flint."

"Flint? Aren't these stones right then?" Lottie got up.

"I don't think they are, no. I think the scout leader said it had to be a certain sort of stone for the spark to light and you have to use steel against it. I don't know why I didn't remember that before but, to be honest, I'm so tired."

Isobel watched as they went hunting amongst the strand of stones on the shoreline, disappointed that the ones she'd collected weren't good enough. They were gone for ages, heads down, focussed and silent. Everything depended on them finding something that would create a spark. How on earth would they ever be found in this remote spot if they couldn't make a fire? They would have to stay on the island with the ducks as their only company all night long. Isobel remembered the snake. It would be up and about in the morning. She shivered. As she did so, Lottie and Al cheered.

"Have you found one?" Isobel sat Lily down near their first attempt at making a fire, as Lottie and Al returned and crouched around the stones.

"Yes, this should do it."

"Is it dry enough, Al?" Lottie peered at the stone in his hand.

"Have to be." Al pulled out his pocketknife and pulled the blade open with his thumbnail.

"Is that new, Al?" Lottie looked impressed.

Al smiled. His teeth showed white against his dirty face. "Had it for my thirteenth birthday from Mum and Dad. Best present I ever had. Let's hope it can do the trick now."

Al and Lottie sat back down next to Lily and Isobel. They all craned their necks to watch as Al struck the steel blade against the flint time after time. Still nothing.

"It's not going to work." Al sat back and let his hands fall.

Lottie took the stone and knife from him. "It's got to work, Al. We'll never get rescued if people can't find us. We've got to keep trying." Lottie struck the knife against the stone and Al hunched over it, his hands full of tinder. After at least ten minutes, when it looked like Lottie had also failed, a spark finally shot out between the stone and the metal blade.

"Again, Lottie! Quickly now." Al held the nest of tinder even closer.

Isobel could see how tired Lottie was. "You can do it, Lottie, keep going!"

Then another spark, a bigger one, flew out towards the dry grass Al held so close to it.

"Blow gently, Al." Lottie sat back, looking exhausted.

To Isobel's immense relief, she saw a minute plume of smoke rising from Al's cupped hands as he blew air across it.

"Do it again, Al." Isobel said, her eyes totally focussed on the bundle of dry grass and lichen.

Al blew a little more forcefully and this time, a tiny flame burst into life.

"Hurray!" All three of them chorused together.

"What's happening?" Lily, now fully conscious, peered across Isobel.

Isobel gathered the little girl into her arms. Lily was shivering violently, and her teeth chattered together. Alarmed, Isobel settled her between her legs. "Look, Lily. Your clever brother has got a fire going. You're going to be lovely and warm very soon."

Al smiled at Isobel and then at his sister. "Don't worry, Lily. We'll soon have a good old blaze going, you'll see."

Lily started to whimper. "I want to go home. I don't want to be here. I'm cold."

Isobel stroked Lily's hair, still damp from the lake. "The fire will show people where we are, Lily, don't you see? Look over there." Isobel pointed at her home. "See all the lights on in the big house? They'll be looking for us and once the fire gets going, it'll be like a beacon and they'll soon find us and take us back home. Everything's going to be alright."

Isobel looked up. Al was gazing at her, his eyes soft and grateful. She hugged Lily to her.

Lottie was adding more twigs to the miniature fire and making it bloom. Soon they all put little bits of wood on and the small flames reached up towards the stars.

"Let's all make a wish." Lottie said.

Surely, Isobel thought desperately, oh, surely, someone will see it and rescue us?

CHAPTER TEN
Lottie

Lottie blew harder on the heart of the fire and the flames answered her plea with a deep red glow. She'd added more sticks, too many, and they were damp, creating thick, black smoke that made the others choke and cough.

She cursed herself for a fool, too eager to create a beacon for the adults at the manor house who must, by now, be anxious and out searching for them. A big fire, easily seen from the grounds or even from inside the house, was their only hope of discovery.

"I'm going for more wood." It was the only way she could salve her conscience for almost dowsing the fire with damp timber.

Al looked up as she stood up. "Make sure it's dry, this time."

Lottie, hurt, walked away, her naked foot relaying what lay underneath it. Lottie pulled off her one shoe. It was easier walking with two bare feet, and her shoe was still soaking wet anyway. The first stars shone in the blackest of skies. She tried to remember what phase of the moon they were in but was too bone weary to work it out. She prayed for a full moon to light her way in the pitch dark. She moved away from the others in search of dry sticks, determined to find only tinder-dry ones.

She went beyond the little beach where she and Lily had ended up and found a stack of planed timber, placed there ready, presumably, to build a new duck house. Quacks and rustlings from the ducks disturbed by her presence filled the air. Excited, she loaded the small planks into her arms, one by one, until she could barely see over the stack. She almost ran back to the others, stubbing her toes on a tree root on the way and nearly dropping the lot.

50

"Look what I've found!"

Al and Isobel turned around. "Gosh, Lottie, that's wonderful!"

Al got up and ran towards her and took some of the wood from her. "Well done, old thing."

They stoked up the fire and Al put the wood on in the shape of a pyramid. At once, the flames shot up towards the night sky, crackling and spitting out their resinous sap.

Lottie sat back on her heels, gazing at the inferno and then across at the house. Could they see this blaze from there? They had to.

She kept piling on more and more planks of wood. "I think they've been treated with creosote, judging by the smell. That should make it go like a bomb."

"Be careful, Lottie. You'll singe your hair." Isobel cautioned.

"I don't care if I go bald, as long as we get found." Lottie looked across the water again. She had never felt more exhausted in her life. She thought about getting the others to join in another song, but she just didn't have the oomph.

They sat around the fire for another half an hour without any sign of rescue and Lily, lolling against Isobel again, fell back into slumber. Her face in the firelight looked rosy now, Lottie was glad to see, not that ashen look that had frightened her witless before.

She kept looking at the lit windows in her home, willing someone to look back at her, praying they would. She was just thinking she'd have to go back for more duck house planks when she saw a different sort of light, a pinprick in the dark, swaying from side to side.

She screwed her eyes up to see better, held her breath. Then she stood up, picked up a burning plank and waved it wildly, running to the water's edge as she did so.

"Lottie! What are you doing? You'll burn yourself!" Isobel's voice receded as Lottie shouted out. "We're here! We're here! Over here on the duck island. Hello, hello?"

"Can you see someone?" Al was by her side. He too brought a flaming stick and was waving it and jumping up and down at the same time.

"Yes! Look! There are men, I can see about three of them, I think. Over there!" Lottie pointed with her firebrand.

Al turned to her. "Yes, yes! I can see them." He started shouting too. "Help! Over here!"

Lottie could hear voices now, though she couldn't make out the words. Gruff men's voices, urgent and low. Then the men started shouting too and other lights streamed down from the house until there were at least half a dozen lanterns.

A lump formed in Lottie's throat. She refused to cry and swallowed it down. She looked back at the bonfire. Lily had woken up, a sleepy smile on her little face. Isobel was helping her to get up. Lottie turned back to the men searching for them. She could make out figures now, the odd glimpse of a face, anxious and strained. There was Andrews, the butler, and ancient George Phipps, the retired head gardener, his bald head shining in the light of his lantern, held high on a shepherd's crook.

The men gathered on the lake's edge opposite the duck island.

"Miss Charlotte? Are you there?" Andrews' Scottish lilt was unmistakable.

"Yes, yes, it's me!" Lottie screamed the words.

"Are you alright?"

"Yes, we're fine!" Lottie yelled back.

"How many of you are there?" Andrews had put his hands to his mouth so she could hear him better.

"Isobel's here with Al and Lily Phipps, from the garage."

"And you're all alright?"

"Yes, but we want to go home!" Lottie's voice broke as the desire to be safe and dry overwhelmed her.

"Stay there. We're coming!" There were mutterings amongst the men. Lottie heard snatches of random words - 'boathouse', 'oars', 'telephone' - exchanged between them. Two men turned and started running back to the house while others went further round the lake, towards the boathouse. Andrews and George Phipps, Al's grandfather, stood patiently at the water's edge.

Lottie turned back to the others. She could not prevent the tears from running down her face this time. "They've found us. We're going to be rescued!"

"Hear that, Lily? Everything's going to be alright." Isobel came forward with Lily and clutched Lottie's hand.

Al hunched his shoulders. "We'll be rescued alright, but there will be hell to pay for this."

"I won't let you take all the blame, Al." Lottie was determined on that point. "We're in this together. Of course, what we should have done was leave a note explaining where we were going. Oh, this morning seems such a long time ago!"

CHAPTER ELEVEN

Al

"You had no right to go off like that, Albert George Phipps. Telling no-one where you were going, I've never known the like. Don't you know how dangerous rivers can be?" Al had never seen his grandfather look so angry.

He hung his head as they walked back to the manor house across the grounds while his grandfather's words rained down on him. The men had quickly found another rowing boat and reached the island. He'd been so relieved that the girls were safe, all he had felt on the boat was gratitude and an overwhelming sense of fatigue. Now, his grandfather left him in no doubt of his shame.

By the time they reached the big house, there was quite a welcoming party gathered on the terrace at the front. On catching sight of them, first his mother, then his father tore down the terrace steps, arms outstretched, faces tight with emotion.

"Oh, thank God, you're all safe." Katy Phipps hugged each of them in turn, Lily first, then Lottie and Isobel, before she finally turned to Al.

"I could murder you, my lad."

No hug for him, then.

"I left you in charge, didn't I? Why didn't you tell anyone where you were headed? No-one gave you permission to take the boat out, did they? I know I certainly didn't. We've been frantic with worry. Look at little Lily, she's half dead!"

Jem, his father, had lifted Lily into his arms and held her against his chest with his good hand. His face was as stern as Al had ever seen it. "I'm ashamed and disappointed in you, Al. You were lucky none of you was drowned. I've a good mind to give you a hiding when we get home. It's no more than you deserve. How old are you? Two, three? No, you are thirteen years old! Why, some boys are down a mine at that age, working like men. And you'll be working too, from now on when you're not at school. No more playing around and heading off who knows where. I'm never letting you out of my sight again."

His mother had an arm around each of the Flintock-Smythe girls and was propelling them up the terrace steps. She turned around at her husband's words and looked at Al. To his astonishment, she gave him a conspiratorial wink and blew him a kiss. Jem had turned away to say something to his father, George, and didn't notice. Although Al was surprised at his mother's sympathy, he was immensely grateful for it and tears pricked the backs of his eyes at the thought that, in her, he had someone close who understood his need for adventure.

They all trooped into the hall and Al's heart took another dive.

Lady Smythe was standing in the centre of the impressive space, with the grand staircase rising behind her, as if she was a judge, or perhaps God, about to deliver his fate.

Al blinked in the bright electric light inside the manor house. They had electricity at the bungalow but not great big chandeliers like these. Their brilliance was dazzling after the deep dark of the duck island and the long plod on weary legs up the hill to Cheadle Manor, lit only by the feeble candlelight of lanterns and torch beams. He couldn't focus his eyes for a few moments and stood, his mouth open and his brain befuddled. Someone, he had no idea who but suspected his father, pushed him to stand in front of the lady of the house. Lady Smythe had raised herself above the crowd gathered in front of her by stepping onto the second stair of the wide staircase. One beringed, plump hand rested on the curved and polished banister. The diamonds in the rings caught the bright light and flashed darts of more brilliance.

She turned first to Lottie and Isobel who were standing to one side of the group. "Charlotte and Isobel. You are to go straight to Mrs Andrew's room. She has my instructions for your welfare. You are very dirty and you both need a hot bath."

"But Granny…" Lottie stepped towards her grandmother.

"I will brook no argument, Charlotte. You are lucky I am not punishing you for this disastrous episode. Your misconduct was a grave error of judgement. I am both surprised and deeply disappointed in you." Lady Smythe pursed her lips.

"I know you're right, and I just wanted to say that it *is* my fault too. I'm older than Al, after all, and I should have left a note or telephoned, or something." Lottie's pleaded to the old woman.

"As I understand it, you were the guest of Albert Phipps and left in the care of his mother. You are not to blame. Now, go, and for heaven's sake, clean yourself up!" Lady Smythe turned towards Al and Lottie and Isobel were bundled away by their butler, Andrews, towards the servants' quarters. Both girls looked round at him and gave tired smiles in sympathy before they disappeared behind the green baize door.

Al felt completely exposed, standing in front of the gathering with Lady Smythe looking down her beaky nose at him, and him alone.

"I should have known something like this would happen," Lady Smythe began. Her voice, as ever, was loud and strident. "You are just like your mother." She looked away from him then, over his head to someone behind. Al turned around. His mother looked unrepentant, even angry. Catching his glance, she came to stand beside him. She held Al's hand as Lady Smythe returned to her speech.

"Look at the two of you. You might resemble your father in looks, Albert Phipps, but you have the arrogance and presumption of your mother. Oh yes, hold the child's hand. You would have done better to smack it more often. No doubt, you approve of this dangerous escapade? And my girls were in your care. Cassandra left them with *you*. What have you to say for yourself, Katherine Phipps, as you now are?"

Al heard his mother's intake of breath, felt the tremble in her hand, still enfolding his own. He squeezed hers and looked up at her. Katy's face was set hard, the jaw clenched, the chin forward. When she spoke, her voice was as strong as Lady Smythe's. In that, at least, they were equals.

"Lady Smythe, I take full responsibility for what has happened. I was the adult in charge and it's not fair to blame my son. I'm sorry that your girls were placed in danger, as I am sure Albert is too. He will be punished accordingly but not by you; we will do it in our own way. I'm sure he has done everything he could to prevent any harm coming to the children and I'm very sorry that I didn't take better care of them."

"But they *have* come to harm, haven't they? I've had a report from one of the men about what happened. You only had to look at them – they could have drowned, for heaven's sake! They're all filthy, bedraggled and bruised. They look like common street urchins. No doubt they are starving hungry too. How dare *you* decide what to do with your son? He should be sent before the magistrate and sentenced, if you ask me. And he's not the only one who should be punished. I shall put word out to boycott your garage, do you hear me? And that disgusting rubber factory of yours. I know people. I have connections to government, both local and national. I shall see to it that you are blacklisted from now on by anyone worth knowing. Cassandra trusted you to take responsibility for these innocent girls of hers." Lady Smythe descended the two stairs that elevated her above the throng.

She walked up to Katy and thrust her face in Al's mother's. Al held his mother's hand even more tightly. He didn't flinch and neither did she.

Lady Smythe's eyes had narrowed into slits. "I will see you ruined for this, you wretched girl. You were always insolent, ungrateful and above yourself. Well, I will see you brought down to your proper level now!"

Al heard a collective gasp of shock from the people standing behind him.

Jem came forward then, and stood next to his wife, Lily still in his arms, her eyes wide and full of fear. "I think you've said enough, Lady Smythe. This is just a thoughtless childish scrape. Any child with spirit is bound to have a few adventures at some point, but I will not have you speaking to my wife like this."

"How dare you address me in such terms, young man! Why, you were nothing but an undergardener here at Cheadle Manor!"

Katy looked straight at her old employer. "But we are not your servants now. We are people with our own business and livelihood, who are hardworking and respected in our community. We do not need your patronage. Tell whoever you like about us. Go on, I dare you! All anyone of 'worth', as you so crudely put it, will think is that you are a vindictive, spiteful old woman who takes out her bitterness on innocent children who were just trying to have fun! Now, I suggest you stop haranguing all of us and see to their care, which is what I am going to do with mine. It's been a long and difficult day, not least for them, but they will recover from this, and they will have learned a lot from their experiences which, no doubt, will stand them in good stead when they become adults. I just hope you don't poison their minds first with your sour, nasty and, frankly, old-fashioned attitude."

"Outrageous woman!" Lady Smythe came even closer, so their faces almost touched. "Know this, madam. Neither you, nor your husband, and certainly not your children, are ever to come through that door again. Do you hear me? Never! I will not have any of you polluting these grounds on any part of the estate. From this moment on, you are *all* banished from Cheadle Manor, and for evermore, this time."

Katy turned to Jem, who still held a wide-eyed Lily in the crook of his good arm, and Al. "Come on, you lot. Let's go home and sort you out."

She nodded to the other servants gathered around them in various stages of shock and disbelief.

Al never let go of his mother's hand as they walked out of Cheadle Manor Hall and down the terrace steps. Neither said anything but Al felt a bond with her that he knew now would never be broken, whatever happened in the future.

At the foot of steps, as they plunged back into the black, moonless night, he looked back. Lady Smythe stood alone in the brightly lit doorway, the electric chandelier illuminating her from behind. The light spilled out in a yellow column onto the terrace and flowed down its steps.

Away from its searchlight, they turned as one, and climbed into their family car.

Lily clung to her father, who sat in the front passenger seat, next to his wife. Al sat alone on the back seat, completely spent.

Katy pressed the ignition button and the engine thrummed into life. "I'm sorry I didn't take better care of you, Al, I really am. It's a lesson for me, too, not to put work before my family. This is more my fault than yours. You should have asked my permission before taking a boat out on the river without a grown-up, it's true. But, if I had been checking on you and hadn't told you not to bother me, none of this would have happened. I'll forgive you, if you'll forgive me?"

"You're not going to tell me off?" Al couldn't believe his ears.

"No, son, we're not going to do that, whatever Lady Smythe says." His father turned around and smiled at him.

His mother nodded. "That's right, Al. I think we've both learned a hard lesson today, haven't we? It's one neither of us will ever forget and remembering the danger you were all in will be punishment enough. Now, let's get home."

The car entered the dark avenue of the driveway, pierced only by the two beams from its headlights. Al leaned back against the seat, thinking about what his parents had said. They were right, he would never forget this day and how close he and the others had come to never seeing another. His mother drove his family away from Cheadle Manor, away from Al's closest friends.

His parents might have forgiven him already, but would he ever see Lottie and Isobel again?

CHAPTER TWELVE
Isobel

Isobel woke the next morning from the deepest sleep of her short life. She ached all over and had a terrific thirst.

She rang the bell for the maid. Ten minutes later, she was surprised to see her mother enter the room, carrying her breakfast tray.

"Mummy!"

"Hello, darling." Cassandra put down the tray on the side table and came and sat on the bed beside her.

"How did you get here from London so quickly?"

"I came on the milk train this morning at dawn. I'd left my car at the station at Woodbury, so it was ready and waiting for me. Easy, really." Cassandra gave her a glass of milk.

Isobel wondered if it had been on the train with her mother and drank it down greedily.

"My, you are thirsty." Cassandra took the empty glass and returned it to the tray. "How are you this morning?"

"I'm fine, Mummy. Just a bit achy, that's all. Is Lottie awake?"

"No, she's still fast asleep. You had quite a day of it yesterday, didn't you?"

Isobel nodded, waiting for an interrogation.

She didn't have to wait long. Her mother buttered some toast for her. The trouble with that was, it was always cold when she had it in bed. Isobel much preferred to go downstairs for breakfast but now wasn't the time to say so.

"So, Bella, whose idea was it exactly to take a boat out on the river, unsupervised?"

Isobel munched her toast, wondering what to say that wouldn't get anyone, especially Al, into trouble. She swallowed it down. "It was all of us together."

"Are you sure?"

"Yes, of course. Aunt Katy was busy in the factory making some new thing that was very important, she said."

"So, Aunt Katy didn't know about your going to the river?"

Isobel shook her head, swallowed some more toast. "No, she told us not to bother her, you see, so we just decided to take a picnic to the river and take the boat out. We never meant to go so far."

"And no-one thought to leave a note at least?" Cassandra poured herself a cup of tea from a small pot on the tray.

"We should have done. We know that now, both Lottie and Al wished they had but we never thought about it. We were all excited, you see. Al said we could pretend we were pirates and we had so much to carry and everything, we just forgot. I took the lemonade and the stoppers stayed in because I carried the bottles so carefully, but we forgot them when the wasps were after us."

"Wasps as well? Oh dear, I'm glad you weren't stung again – you weren't, were you?"

Isobel shook her head.

"Well, that's a relief at least." Cassandra sipped her tea. "It's unlike Lottie not to let people know what she's up to. It was so irresponsible of her, of both of you."

"I know, but when Aunt Katy forbade us to bother her, we sort of felt free, you know, as if we could do what we liked, and she wouldn't care as long as we left her alone." Isobel was pleased she'd found a way of explaining without getting Al into trouble.

Her mother looked flushed. She stood up and went to the window. "Aunt Katy actually said not to bother her all day, did she?"

"Yes, that's right, Mummy. She said she had to concentrate really hard. Uncle Jem was out and so was Mr Bradbury, their manager. Only Mr Threadwell was there, and he was busy serving customers for petrol. So, we were quite alone." It was working. Al wouldn't get the blame now!

"And, am I right in thinking you went through the sluice gate to the lake in that boat and it capsized?"

"Oh, Mummy, it was terrifying! Lily almost drowned, you know, but Lottie saved her, and Al helped me swim to the island. He was so clever at making a fire too. He'd learned how in the scouts. We gathered wood, well, I got the stones because of the snake, and it took ages, but he got it going with his pen knife and a different stone in the end! Wasn't that good of him?"

"There was a snake? Goodness me! Perhaps it *was* good of Al to build a fire, otherwise you might never have been found, but it's a pity his thoughtlessness put you in danger in the first place." Her mother was pacing now, up and down the room, restless and deep in thought.

"Bella, you'll have to excuse me now, there's something I simply must do. You stay in bed as long as you want this morning, darling. And I want to know if you feel unwell at any time, do you hear me? If you feel you're running a temperature or feel dizzy or anything, you're to ring the bell for Andrews. I'm going to telephone Dr Benson to come over and do a check up on both you girls, so stay in bed until he's been. Do you understand?"

Isobel nodded, not quite sure of her mother's mood. She looked odd, sort of angry.

"I'm going downstairs now, and I might be out for a while. I should be back by lunchtime. You can play quietly in the nursery, once the doctor's seen you, until I return. Don't bother Granny – not at all – alright?"

"Yes, Mummy, if you say so."

"I do. Now, finish your breakfast. I'll take a look at Lottie, make sure she's alright, and then I'm going to pay someone a visit."

"Who?"

But her mother had gone.

It was lunchtime before she saw her again. Dr Benson had inspected them and told both the girls there was nothing wrong with them beyond a few bruises and they should get up and forget all about it.

Heeding her mother's warning, Isobel stayed in the nursery with Lottie. She was more than happy to leave her grandmother in peace and dreaded an encounter with her. Isobel thought they'd got off very lightly the night before but was confident she hadn't heard the last of a lecture about yesterday's antics. In fact, neither she, nor Lottie, knew what else had been said to the others. She hoped Granny hadn't been too hard on poor Al and felt guilty he'd had to face the music alone, but at least his parents had been with him.

Isobel glanced across at Lottie who was sitting in her favourite window seat reading a book. She had a big bruise on her forehead that was slowing turning purple. No wonder Lottie had passed out by the lakeside.

Isobel lost herself in a jigsaw. It was one she'd done before, so she didn't have to think too hard. She was much too tired to do that.

"Oh, there's the gong for lunch." Lottie looked up from her book.

"Good, I'm hungry." Isobel got up from the table.

Downstairs, they found Lady Smythe in the formal dining room. "Oh dear," Lottie whispered to her, "Granny looks very peevish."

Isobel walked into the room behind her sister. Lottie wasn't afraid of anything, but Isobel dreaded a sermon from her grandmother.

"Hello, Granny. How are you today?" Lottie gave their grandmother an over-bright smile but received not even a hint of one in return.

"Sit down, girls. Where is your mother?"

Isobel was glad Lottie answered for them both. "Mummy said she had to go out this morning."

"Did she say where?" Lady Smythe picked up her linen napkin and withdrew it from its silver holder.

"No, sorry, she didn't." Lottie glanced at Isobel, who sat opposite her. "Did she tell you where she was going, Bella?"

"Um, no…no, she didn't." Bella placed her napkin on her lap.

Just then, their mother entered the room. She looked most upset and still wore her hat, the one with the blue peacock feather and she had her matching blue coat on too, but it was buttoned all wrong.

"Cassandra! Remove your headwear before joining us, please." Lady Smythe frowned.

"Oh, never mind my damn hat, Mother." Cassandra sat down at the other end of the table and drew off her gloves.

"Really! Cassandra – no swearing in front of the girls." Lady Smythe's frown deepened.

"It's the girls I want to talk about." Cassandra unpinned her hat and threw it on the sideboard. It's metal brooch, the one that held the feather in place, pinged against the silver urn, making a loud noise before falling to the floor.

Andrews went to pick it up.

Cassandra looked at him. "Leave it, Andrews, it doesn't matter. And leave us alone for a moment. Oh, and shut the door, would you?"

"But luncheon is served, madam." Andrews looked most put out.

"Never mind the food. This shouldn't take long. Come back in ten minutes." Cassandra waved him away.

"Very good, madam." Andrews left the room as silently as only he could. The double doors closed softly behind him.

"What is this about, Cassandra? What is it you have to say that can't be said in front of Andrews?" Lady Smythe, Isobel knew from experience, hated any delay to a meal.

Cassandra got up and strode about the room. She went to the window and looked out for a moment. Then she turned and faced her children and her mother.

Isobel's heart began to beat fiercely. She had a feeling that what was going to happen next would somehow be awful.

"Well, Mother, girls…I've just been down to The Katherine Wheel Garage to see Katy and Jem Phipps." Cassandra paced again. Isobel wished her mother would sit down. She'd never seen her so agitated.

Isobel stole a glance at Lottie who looked as apprehensive as she felt.

Their mother took a deep breath. "I understand that you have banished Al and Lily from Cheadle Manor, Mother?"

Lady Smythe chipped in. "That's right, and their parents too. Jumped up servants should never have been allowed in as guests in the first place, if you ask me."

Cassandra scowled at her mother. "You know my feelings on that, Mother. You know I believe in equality. Kate and Jem are my friends – or they were. Having said that, no doubt you will be pleased to know that I actually agree with your decree on them not visiting the manor again."

"What?" Lottie jumped up from her chair.

66

Isobel couldn't believe her ears. She didn't know anything about whatever her mother called it – a decree? What did that mean?

Cassandra came forward and leant her hands on the polished table and looked at each of them in turn. "I have never been so angry in all my life as when Isobel told me that Kate had let the children look after themselves yesterday. She had not bothered to check on them once. She didn't even know they'd gone down to the river! How dare she put my girls in danger when I left you in her care?"

Isobel stared at her mother, hardly able to believe what she was saying. "But Mummy, we were only playing. We're alright now."

Lottie nodded. "Yes, Mummy. No harm done. There's no need to banish the Phipps family!"

"I will decide who comes here, Lottie, not you." Cassandra stood upright again. "Don't you see, girls?" A sob escaped her. "You're all I have left of your dear father! All I have left of my beloved Douglas."

Isobel jumped up and went to her mother's side. Cassandra had broken down into heaving sobs. Isobel put her arms around her mother's thin frame.

"Oh, don't cry, Mummy, please, don't cry! We won't ever be naughty again." Isobel couldn't think of anything more grown up to say. It was so distressing to see her mother cry.

Lottie didn't join in the hug. "It's ridiculous to banish our friends. I'm going to my room."

Lottie almost wrenched the door off its hinges and banged it shut behind her. Isobel, torn between consoling her sister and mother, didn't know what to do.

Lady Smythe made the decision for her. "Isobel, go upstairs with your sister. I need to talk to your mother. I'll have something sent up to the nursery for your lunch."

Isobel hesitated.

"I said, leave us, Isobel!" Lady Smythe pointed at the door.

"Mummy?"

Cassandra nodded, still crying. "It's probably best, Bella. I'll…I'll see you later, darling."

Isobel let her arms drop to her sides and followed her sister out of the room. She found Lottie in the nursery. She was holding her favourite old teddy bear to her chest and was nibbling on his torn ear.

"Oh, Lottie! What does it all mean?" Isobel joined her sister on the window seat and burst into tears.

Lottie patted her back and handed her a handkerchief. "It means that we can't ever see Al or Lily or Aunt Katy or Uncle Jem – not ever again."

"But they can't do that! I couldn't bear it if we never saw Al and, um, Lily again." Isobel wiped her eyes and stared at her sister, willing her to come up with some sort of solution.

Lottie looked thoughtful for a moment, then she said, "Not here, anyway."

Isobel stopped crying. A tear dropped off her chin on to the toy bear. "Oh, yes! Mummy only said they couldn't come here."

Lottie grinned. "You're absolutely right! They might not be able to visit us at Cheadle Manor, but no-one has said we can't go there!"

"We can't let the grown-ups win, can we?" Isobel hugged her sister.

Lottie hugged her back hard. "No, we can't. We'll think of a way to see Al and Lily at The Katherine Wheel Garage, and we'll make quite sure no-one but us knows anything about it."

THE END

The Katherine Wheel Series

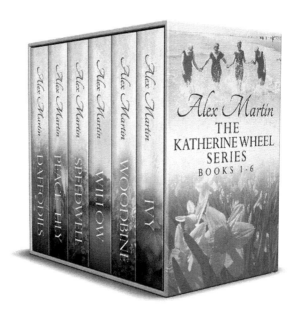

"Excellent novels with a well rounded and strong central female character. You do need to read all the books, but they are all good so go for it and enjoy."

Daffodils is also available as an
AUDIOBOOK
Narrated by the author

Book One of The Katherine Wheel Series

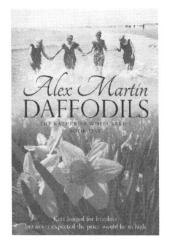

Katy dreams of a better life than just being a domestic servant at Cheadle Manor. Her one attempt to escape is thwarted when her flirtation with the manor's heir results in a scandal that shocks the local community.
Jem Beagle has always loved Katy. His offer of marriage rescues her, but personal tragedy divides them. Jem leaves his beloved Wiltshire to become a reluctant soldier on the battlefields of World War One. Katy is left behind, restless and alone.
Lionel White, just returned from being a missionary in India, brings a dash of colour to the small village, and offers Katy a window on the wider world.
Katy decides she has to play her part in the global struggle and joins the war effort as a WAAC girl.
She finally breaks free from the stifling Edwardian hierarchies that bind her but the brutality of global war brings home the price she has paid for her search.

"Impressively well-researched and vividly imagined."

"A fantastic story which was written beautifully. I have not read many books based around WW1 and this was just right. The characters have some hard times and I found myself in tears at times, but overall, the story was told in a way I could relate to and understand. Highly recommended for fans of historical fiction."

"Probably one of the best books I've read of this genre. Took me to the First World War as never before. Will certainly read the second with great anticipation. Only chose it because of the price and picture on the front but what a find and such a treat !!!"

"Daffodils is an extraordinary story of commitment and enduring hope which teaches us the power of resilience, integrity and true honor. This book was a deeply emotional experience that managed to reach the inner core of my being. This is such a powerful story! Highly recommended."

Daffodils is also available as an audio book, narrated by the author

Book Two of The Katherine Wheel Series

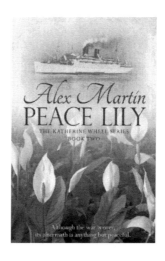

Although the war is over, its aftermath is anything but peaceful

After the appalling losses suffered during World War One, three of its survivors long for peace, unaware that its aftermath will bring different, but still daunting, challenges.

Katy trained as a mechanic during the war and cannot bear to return to the life of drudgery she left behind. A trip to America provides the dream ticket she has always craved and an opportunity to escape the straitjacket of her working-class roots. She jumps at the chance, little realising that it will change her life forever, but not in the way she'd hoped.

Jem lost not only an arm in the war, but also his livelihood, and with it, his self-esteem. How can he keep restless Katy at home and provide for his wife? He puts his life at risk a second time, attempting to secure their future and prove his love for her.

Cassandra has fallen deeply in love with Douglas Flintock, an American officer she met while driving ambulances at the Front. How can she persuade this modern American to adapt to her English country way of life, and all the duties that come with inheriting Cheadle Manor? When Douglas returns to Boston, unsure of his feelings, Cassandra crosses the ocean, determined to lure him back.

As they each try to carve out new lives, their struggles impact on each other in unforeseen ways.

"Daffodils' sequel Peace Lily is as enthralling and fresh as its predecessor."

"Great follow on book. Couldn't put down till finished."

Book Three of The Katherine Wheel Series

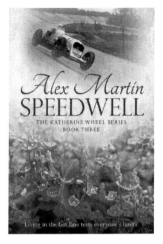

Living in the fast lane tests everyone's limits

Katy and Jem enter the 1920's with their future in the balance. How can they possibly make their new enterprise work? They must risk everything, including disaster, and trust their gamble will pay off.

Cassandra, juggling the demands of a young family, aging parents and running Cheadle Manor, distrusts the speed of the modern age, but Douglas races to meet the new era, revelling in the freedom of the open road.

Can each marriage survive the strain the new dynamic decade imposes? Or will the love they share deepen and carry them through? They all arrive at destinies that surprise them in Speedwell, the third book in the Katherine Wheel Series.

"I really enjoyed the stories. Read all three books in the series while on holiday. Her writing style makes for comfortable reading. Her characters are credible and in the main her story lines are unpredictable and powerfully descriptive."

"A fascinating set of characters weave their magical story through a daring enterprise just after the end of the Great War. The story travels from humble but daring

beginnings in a small Wiltshire village with Katy and Jem and takes us to Boston in the USA and back."
Book Four of The Katherine Wheel Series

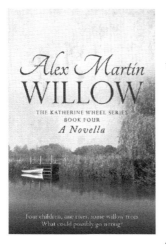

Willow is a short novella that bridges the generational gap. Book Four in The Katherine Wheel Series may be small, but it packs in many surprises for the children of Katy and Jem, and Douglas and Cassandra.

"This is a very well written and descriptive novella with the children and the idyllic countryside setting, well observed and portrayed. You feel you are there experiencing it first-hand. It draws you into a totally believable world, perfect material for a film or a Sunday evening drama series."

"This tale brings to life their distinctive well-rounded characters; the dialogue distinguishes each child's voice and fits exactly into the era it represents. The descriptive narrative sets the scene perfectly and moves the plot along in gripping speed."

The stifling heat of a midsummer's day lures four children to the cool green waters of the river that runs between Cheadle Manor and The Katherine Wheel Garage.
Al captains the little band of pirates as they blithely board the wooden dinghy. Headstrong Lottie vies with him to be in charge while Isobel tries to keep the peace and look after little Lily.

But it is the river that is really in control.

Lost and alone, the four children must face many dangers, but it is the unforeseen consequences of their innocent adventure that will shape their futures for years to come.

Book Five of The Katherine Wheel Series

Two sisters, divided by love and war, must each fight a different battle to survive

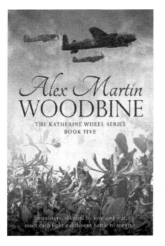

Lottie, her sister Isobel and Al, the man they both love, are on the brink of adulthood and the Second World War in Woodbine, the fifth book in The Katherine Wheel Series. Trapped and alone in occupied France, Lottie must disguise her identity and avoid capture if she is to return and heal the bitter feud over the future of Cheadle Manor.

Back in England, Al is determined to prove himself. He joins the Air Transport Auxiliary service, flying aeroplanes to RAF bases all over the country.

Isobel defies everyone's expectations by becoming a Land Girl. Bound by a promise to a dying woman, she struggles to break free and follow her heart.

"Great story - this is a real family saga through the important milestones of the 20th Century. It's all here. Love, hate, life, death, war and peace. Woodbine takes us through the second world war with real insight into people's lives. I especially enjoyed Lottie's time in France and the scenes in the Normandy farmhouse are very evocative. Looking forward to the next, and final, chapter to see how everything comes together."

"Woodbine is fifth book of the brilliant Katherine Wheel series and, having read and enjoyed all four of the previous books I was looking forward to this one. I was not disappointed; Alex Martin has once again brought to life the characters that I followed all that time and, I have to say, I've been riveted by the historic detail to the background of the stories. It is obvious that the author researches extensively to portray the atmosphere of each era – and succeeds again with Woodbine."

"This is Book 5 in the series and carries on with the next generation of Katy and Cassandra, both ladies from different spectrum of the social classes have a deep and abiding friendship. Now their children are grown and are now encountering WWII. Surprises of inheritance, a love triangle, and the turmoil of a world war. I've read all the previous books and would advise a reader to start with the first book so that they get the full impact of these two families. Well written, well researched."

IVY

Book Six in The Katherine Wheel Series

Two sisters, each caught in a trap in World War Two, must escape to find their true destiny

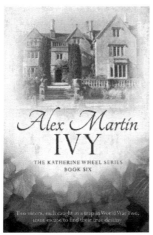

All the disparate threads of this epic saga are seamlessly woven together in Ivy, the sixth and final book in The Katherine Wheel Series.

Drawn into the Resistance in Occupied France, Lottie's strengths and endurance are tested to the limit.

Home-loving Isobel, torn between love and duty, must set herself free if she is ever to find happiness.

Flying planes for the Air Transport Auxiliary frequently puts Al in danger but securing the woman he loves proves much more challenging.

Cheadle Manor once lay at the heart of the lives of Lottie, Isobel and Al, but World War Two has broken every bond tying them to their safe haven. Can they ever come home and be together again?

"5.0 out of 5 stars A majestic Series finale: a perfectly paced drama, full of tension, mystery,

I love this beautifully woven story of Ivy, the impressive conclusion of the Katherine Wheel Series. It is so easy to visualise how it could have felt being Lottie in wartime occupied France. She has to draw on her huge courage to face some very scary exploits, whilst her friends there also risked their lives to help bring freedom to Europe. It's such a satisfying read, as the array of interesting characters pull us into into life from their perspective in France as well as rural England through their own adventures. Gripping at times, I really wanted to know how things would turn out for everyone - the families and friends in Wiltshire, her friends in France - and especially Lottie herself. The ending is excellent!
romance and compassion."

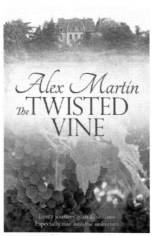

Every journey is an adventure. Especially one into the unknown.
The shocking discovery of her lover with someone else propels Roxanne into escaping to France and seeking work

as a grape-picker. She's never been abroad before and certainly never travelled alone.

Opportunistic loner, Armand, exploits her vulnerability when they meet by chance. She didn't think she would see him again or be the one who exposes his terrible crime.

Join Roxanne on her journey of self-discovery, love and tragedy in rural France. Taste the wine, feel the sun, drive through the Provencal mountains with her, as her courage and resourcefulness are tested to the limit.

The Twisted Vine is set in the heart of France and is a deeply romantic but suspenseful tale. Roxanne Rudge escapes her cheating boyfriend by going grape picking in France. She feels vulnerable and alone in such a big country where she can't speak the language and is befriended by Armand le Clair, a handsome Frenchman. Armand is not all he seems, however, and she discovers a darker side to him before uncovering a dreadful secret. She is aided and abetted by three new friends she has made, charming posh Peter, a gifted linguist; the beautiful and vivacious Italian, Yvane; and clever Henry of the deep brown eyes with the voice to match. Together they unravel a mystery centred around a beautiful chateau and play a part in its future.

"The original setting of this novel and the beauty of colorful places that Roxanne visits really drew me in. This book was a lot more than I'd expected, because aside from the romantic aspect, there's a great deal of humor, fantastic friendship, and entertaining dialogue. I strongly recommend this book to anyone who likes women's fiction."

"This is a wonderful tale told with compassion, emotion, thrills and excitement and some unexpected turns along the way. Oh, and there may be the smattering of a romance in there as well! Absolutely superb."

<u>The Rose Trail</u> is a time slip story set in both the English Civil War and the present day woven together by a supernatural thread.

Is it chance that brings Fay and Persephone together? Or is it the restless and malevolent spirit who stalks them both?
Once rivals, they must now unite if they are to survive the mysterious trail of roses they are forced to follow into a dangerous, war torn past.

"The past has been well researched although I don't know a lot about this period in history it all rings so true – the characters are fantastic with traits that you like and dislike which also applies to the 'present' characters who have their own issues to contend with as well as being able to connect with the past."

"A combination of love, tragedies, friendships, past and present, lashings of historical aspects, religious bias, controlling natures all combined with the supernatural give this novel a wonderful page-turning quality."

" I loved this book, the storyline greatly appealed to me and the history it contained. Fay has always been able to see spirits. The love of her life is Robin, whom she met when she was 11 at school. She trains to become an accountant and purely by chance meets up with an old school friend. The book develops into an enthralling adventure for them both as they slip back and forth in time."

All Alex Martin's stories are available as ebooks as well as paperbacks and make great gifts!

Alex writes about her work on her blog at
www.intheplottingshed.com
where you can get your FREE copy of Alex Martin's short story collection, 'Trio', by clicking on the picture of the shed.

Constructive reviews oil a writer's wheel like nothing else and are very much appreciated on Amazon or Goodreads or anywhere else!

Alex Martin, Author

Facebook page:
https://www.facebook.com/TheKatherineWheel/
Twitter handle: https://twitter.com/alex_martin8586
Email: alexxx8586@gmail.com

Printed in Great Britain
by Amazon